WAVE

WAVE

D.M. OUELLET

HIP Xtreme Novels

NATIONAL LIBRARY OF CANADA CATALOGUING IN PUBLICATION DATA
Ouellet, Debbie

Wave / Debbie Ouellet.

ISBN 978-1-926847-27-6

I. Title.

PS8629.U33W38 2012 jC813'.6 C2012-901224-6

General editor: Paul Kropp
Text Design: Laura Brady
Illustrations by: Charlie Hnatiuk
Cover design: Robert Corrigan

1 2 3 4 5 6 7 17 16 15 14 13 12

Printed and bound in Canada

High Interest Publishing acknowledges the financial support of the Government of Canada through the Canada Book Fund for our publishing activities.

Luke and Mai could see the tsunami coming at them, but that didn't give them enough time to get away. When the first wave hit, they fought to breathe and somehow reach dry land. Then the second wave hit, and the real disaster began.

Contents

Chapter 1 **Tsunami!** / 3
Chapter 2 **Hold On!** / 12
Chapter 3 **Jump!** / 17
Chapter 4 **Higher Ground** / 23
Chapter 5 **Food and Water** / 30
Chapter 6 **The Dark** / 35
Chapter 7 **The Search** / 43
Chapter 8 **Found and Lost** / 52
Chapter 9 **A Battle** / 59
Chapter 11 **Wall of the Lost** / 65
Chapter 11 **Have You Seen My Mom?** / 72
Chapter 12 **Reunion** / 77

Chapter 1
Tsunami!

I was doing laps in the hotel pool thinking about a fight I'd just had with my mom. She had stormed out of our hotel room, almost crying. I had come down to the pool to calm down.

I looked up to see Mai, the kid who would soon be my sister, standing on the balcony of our room. Mai had her arms crossed in front of her. She kept shouting at me to come back to the room. At least, I think that's what Mai was saying. Sometimes, when Mai gets angry, she forgets to speak English.

I ducked my head under water to muffle the sound of her voice. When I came back up, Mai's voice had changed. I looked up to see Mai pointing out to sea.

She looked scared. Really scared.

That's when I noticed people running. Some were shouting. Some ran toward the sea. Some ran away from it. But all of them were scared of something.

I got out of the pool and climbed onto the diving board for a better look.

Out beyond the beach, something strange was happening to the sea.

I'd seen the tide go out before. But this was different. Now the water had gone out so far that fish were flopping around on the dry ocean floor. Boats had been swept out and smashed into each other. Tourists were racing along the beach. They kept calling to people who had gone out to swim just moments before. Those swimmers were gone.

"Mai, what's happening?" I shouted up to her.

Mai was sobbing and shaking. She pointed to the sea and yelled something in Thai.

"Use English, Mai," I called.

She pounded her fist on the railing as she searched for what to say. Then Mai yelled one word that froze my blood.

"Tsunami!"

People shouted and screamed. They knocked each other down as they jumped from balconies and ran. Some fell to their knees and just stared at the sea. Frozen. They were frozen by fear.

I knew just how they felt. I couldn't move either. I just stood there and watched the huge black wall of water get bigger and bigger. This monster wave was swallowing boats and growing by the minute.

I looked up to see Mai curled up on the balcony. Two thoughts flashed in my mind.

Mai is afraid of the water.

When the tide goes out, it always comes back in.

That mountain of a wave was going to come back to Patong Beach. It was going to come back hard and strong. And when it came back, the wave might just kill us all.

"Luke, help me!"

Mai's cry shook me from my trance. I climbed down from the diving board and raced up to our room. There wasn't time to do much, so I threw on some shorts and shoes. It took me only five minutes to reach Mai. The poor kid was lying on the floor, crying.

I pulled Mai to her feet. "We have to go now!"

Mai looked like she wanted to argue. But I pointed

to the west. The wall of water was enormous. And it was headed our way, dragging broken ships with it. I grabbed Mai's hand and we ran. Inland. Away from the water. Somewhere – anywhere – safe and dry.

I'm a fast runner, but Mai had trouble keeping up.

When I turned to look at her, I could see the water charging at us. "Don't look back," I shouted to her, but really to myself.

We could hear the wave coming as we ran.

Behind us, I could hear people screaming. I ignored my own advice and stole a look behind me. People were being sucked into the giant wave.

I didn't look back again.

Just keep running, I told myself.

I could feel the wave rushing right behind me. I kept telling myself that I could outrun it. But my legs ached and my lungs felt like they'd explode. And there was Mai. She wasn't in shape like me. Mai kept stumbling, holding me back.

Just. Keep. Running.

My mind told me it would be so much easier without Mai. The water had reached our ankles. It was harder to run from it with her dragging me back. And now, the wave was more than just water. Tree branches, chairs, pieces broken from buildings – they were all being carried along by the wave. They came streaming right beside us.

The water roared like an angry animal as it forced its way through the streets. I could feel it tugging at my legs. Trying to pull me down.

In another minute, the water was at our waists and I couldn't run anymore. Mai screamed as the wave ripped her hand from mine.

"Luke! Help me, Luke!" Mai thrashed in the water until a branch knocked against her. Then Mai went under.

"MAI!"

I dove into the wave and swam like I never have before. It was hard. The water wanted to pull me with it. I almost panicked when I saw what the wave was dragging through the streets with it. Bodies. Everywhere. Their blank eyes stared back at me as I searched frantically through the water for Mai.

Don't think about it! I told myself. *You can't help them. Maybe you can help Mai.*

Then I saw Mai's bright yellow T-shirt below me. Mai had her arms wrapped around the branch that hit her. Thank goodness it slowed her down enough for me to catch up . . . if I could swim hard enough. Every muscle in me was screaming from the effort. Still, I put on one more burst of speed until I reached her.

I grabbed Mai by the hair to pull her up above the water. I knew she was going to end up with a serious headache from that, but it was the only thing I could get a good grip on. And my lungs were about to burst. If I didn't get my head above water soon, we were both going down for good.

I took a moment to tread water and catch my breath. Mai's head was leaning against me, but she wasn't moving.

I really needed to rest. But I looked around and knew the truth. If I didn't get moving right away, we'd both be dead. Cars, trucks, buses . . . they were all being swept along with the wave. And they were heading straight for us.

Can I outswim them? I judged the distance to a nearby hotel. I could see where a third floor balcony jutted just above the water. It looked like it was still safe. Then my heart sank. No way was I going to make it, especially with Mai like a dead weight in my arms.

Dead weight. Don't even think that, I told myself.

I knew I had to think of something fast. Then I

remembered what my old swim coach said. "Life's like a current, if you can't swim against it, try swimming with it. At least until it gets you to where you need to be."

But this "current"? How could the current get me where I needed to be?

A broken tree branch slammed into my back. I grunted and swore. And then the idea came to me.

I grabbed onto a desk that was floating along with the the other junk. The desk slowed us down a little. I put Mai half on, half off the desk. That gave me both hands free. And then I waited.

I had my eye on a big bus floating in the water. It had a flat top a large luggage rack top. The bus would keep us above the water. If we could only get to it.

When the bus was a few yards away, I grabbed hold of Mai's arm. Then I pushed with my feet as hard as I could against the desk. It was just enough to propel us toward the bus.

Mai's weight made it harder. My brain thought about how much easier it would be if I didn't have her to look after. I told it to shut up. Then I reached out with my free hand for the luggage rack on the bus. I missed. I reached out again and grabbed the rack as tightly as I could. Then I got ready. I had one chance to pull both of us up onto the bus.

One chance.

I pulled with all the strength I had, lifting myself up. It felt like my shoulder was being yanked out of its socket. Still, I hooked both feet into the rail on the other side of the bus roof. Then I hauled Mai up.

She lay limp and cold on the bus's roof. I cursed and put my ear down by her mouth.

Mai wasn't breathing.

Chapter 2

Hold On!

At first I froze. "Don't you dare be dead!" I yelled at Mai. As if I could revive her by shouting.

Think, think, think! You know what you're supposed to do, I told myself. I was, after all, a trained lifeguard. Then my CPR training kicked in.

Nothing was easy with the bus moving through the water at breakneck speed. Still, I managed to hook one foot around the luggage rack. Then I wedged Mai up against the railing in front of me. That way I could free my hands.

As I pumped my hands against her chest, I counted the seconds. One, two, three . . . Then I'd stop and try to breath air back into her lungs.

Please don't be dead.

It was hard to think straight. Cars and branches banged into the bus as we rushed along with the water through the street. There were bodies everywhere, swept along with the junk. I tried not to look at them.

Just think about counting the seconds, I told myself. *You can't help those people.*

"Come on, Mai!" My shoulders and elbows ached from the effort of keeping us steady.

It felt like forever, but it was only minutes before Mai's body jerked forward. At first, she coughed up water. Then she panicked. It took all my strength to hold her down as she kicked her arms and legs.

"Let me go!" Mai kept yelling at me. I knew she was in shock as she punched and scratched, but her punches really hurt.

"Mai, stop!" I shook her as hard as I could. "If you don't calm down right now, we're both going to end up back in the water. Is that what you want?"

Mai's eyes grew wide and her mouth fell open. But she stopped thrashing around. Somehow she realized exactly where she was. Mai grabbed hold of the railing and turned onto her stomach to look around.

"How did we get here? All I can remember is being in the water." Mai's body shook as the memory came back to her.

"I pulled you out," I said. "You didn't much like it."

That's when Mai saw the red scratches and bruises forming all along my arms.

"Oh, Luke, did I do that?"

I never had a chance to answer her. There were a

series of thumps against the bus as windows, doors and pieces of buildings slammed into us.

In the midst of all that, I heard a voice call, "Help!" There was only that one word in English. Everything else was in Thai.

Was I really going crazy? All around us I could see dead bodies among the swirling junk. But a voice?

I looked at Mai and realized that she heard it too. "Where are you?" she called. Then, thinking again, she said it in Thai.

The voice replied in English, "Here. Down under you."

I held onto the railing and raised myself to look over the side of the bus.

There he was – a local guy about my age, maybe younger. He was waving one arm. The other arm was frantically trying to latch onto the bus.

"Hold on. I'm coming," I called to him. I unhooked my foot from the luggage rack. Then I pulled my weight along the edge of the bus's roof until I was directly above him.

"Grab hold of my ankles," I told Mai.

When Mai had a good grip on them, I let go of the rail and reached over the side of the bus. It took a few tries, but I managed to grab the guy's hand.

Then I pulled with all my strength. It hurt like crazy. Every muscle screamed from trying to lift the guy's weight. I managed to get him high enough to hold onto one of the railings on the bus roof. I was too tired to pull him any higher.

"Just hold on," I called out to him. "We'll figure something out."

I expected at least a thank you, but he started yelling at me in Thai. I had no idea what he was saying, but his body language told me he was scared. He kept pointing ahead of us with his free hand as he yelled.

Then Mai screamed, "Oh no, Luke! Up ahead!"

Up ahead was a cement overpass. The wave was sending our bus straight toward it. And there was no way the bus was going to fit under it.

Chapter 3

Jump!

We had to move fast. The bus was racing through the water. Any minute, it would slam into the cement overpass that was right in front of us. When it hit, we'd be crushed or thrown back into the water.

I looked at the local boy, hanging on for dear life from the side of the bus. I looked at Mai. And I made a choice.

"Climb on top," I said to the boy as I reached for his hand. He pulled on the railing and I helped him up. Then he lay down on the bus roof beside me.

"We all have to jump," I said to Mai. "You'd better tell this guy in Thai to make sure he understands." I started to explain how our timing had to be just right.

We had to jump up just as the bus was reaching the overpass. But Mai cut me off.

"Jump? Up there? Are you out of your mind?"

"It's either that or get crushed when the bus hits. Would you rather have that happen?"

I think Mai was still in shock. She started to shout at me. "No way! There's got to be something else." She was pounding her fist. "I am not jumping."

It was too much. "Fine!" I yelled back. "Then I'll go without you. Just see how long you'll last without me."

"You wouldn't dare." Mai's eyes narrowed. I was sure at that moment that she hated me.

"Try me," I warned.

I helped the local kid to his feet and tried to explain what I had in mind. There wasn't much time left. We had to jump soon if we were going to make it.

Of course, he didn't understand. He kept shaking his head. Then Mai said something to him in Thai. The boy's eyes grew wide. He looked at me, at the overpass and back again. Finally he nodded and said, "Okay, man."

I reached my hand out to Mai. "We can hold hands when we jump. I promise I won't let you go."

"I thought you were going to leave me behind."

"Don't be stupid. You coming or not?" My mind raced. I'd only said I'd leave her behind to stop her panicking. She was almost my sister, after all. If we stayed where we were, we'd die for sure when the bus hit the overpass.

We had to jump NOW.

Then Mai yelled and grabbed my hand. I tensed my legs and pushed up with all my might. In seconds we were flying through the air. The local boy was right behind us.

I hit the pavement hard. Everything hurt. My head spun and my teeth rattled. I groaned and rolled onto my stomach. I stayed there until the earth stopped spinning around me.

That's when the whole overpass shook and groaned. Cars, tree branches and our bus all slammed into it. I covered my ears and braced myself. Thankfully, the overpass held.

"Mai, you okay?" I called.

"I hurt," she said from a few feet away.

I crawled over to check her injuries. Nothing was broken. She was just bruised and sore like me.

"Kasem," said the local kid. He was kneeling beside us trying to catch his breath.

"What?"

"My name is Kasem." He grinned at me. "Thanks, man."

"No problem," I answered, still gulping air into my lungs. "I'm Luke. This is Mai. Where are you from?"

Kasem looked around him sadly. "Patong Beach," he said. "This is my home."

I got to my feet and looked around. We'd spent so

much time just trying to stay alive that I hadn't seen all the destruction. Looking down from the overpass, it was as if the town had been kicked in the gut. Buildings were destroyed, trees toppled. Cars and trucks were piled on top of each other. Some were floating in the water that remained in the streets. People were hanging from balconies, or wherever they'd found a dry spot to hold onto. I could hear people crying, calling out for loved ones who were missing.

And then there were all those bodies.

My mind went numb from it.

And what about Mom? Is she down there with them? Or did she get away in time? The thought pushed its way into my brain. I tried to shut it out.

Mom will be okay, I told myself. I'd find her somehow. I'd be able to tell her how stupid I was for that fight we had. For trying to get in the way of her happiness. I'd have my chance to say I was sorry.

But that stupid voice kept whispering at the back of my mind. *You sure, Luke? What if the wave got her? What if you never get to tell her?*

I shut the voice out. I had other things to think about. *Count your blessings, Luke,* Mom would always tell me. *Just remember, when things look bad, there's always someone worse off than you.*

I looked around me again and tried to take her advice. Yeah, those people floating face down in the muddy water, they were worse off.

At least Mai and I were alive.

I looked at the survivors who were making their way through the rubble. That's when I saw that the water had retreated from the streets. After the first great wave, everything had gone quiet. Strangely quiet. Then one of the people shouted and everyone started to scream and run again. They were running farther into the town, away from the ocean.

I looked out to the sea and fell to my knees. "Yeah, right. Count your blessings, Luke."

"What do you see?" Mai asked.

I couldn't speak. The water had gone way out into the ocean again. Another giant wave was forming.

And it would be bigger than the last one.

Chapter 4

Higher Ground

"Mai, Kasem . . . get up." I reached for Mai's hand and pulled her to her feet. "We have to get out of here, now."

Mai looked out to the sea and started to cry. "No, no, no. Not again. I don't think I can do this again, Luke." She was shaking all over.

"Sure you can." I tried to comfort her. "We just have to find a way to higher ground before the next wave hits." Mai still looked really scared. I remembered how afraid of the water she had been. I couldn't help but feel sorry for her.

"I can't. . . ."

"Look, I know I was kind of angry before. But I

didn't mean it. I would never leave you behind, Mai. I give you my word."

Mai was still shaking, but she squeezed my hand tightly. "Okay, Luke." She took a deep breath and calmed herself. "I believe you."

Then, I turned toward Kasem. "You know this city, right?"

Mai translated for me and Kasem nodded.

"We need to find some way to get up higher." I pretended to climb a ladder as I talked.

Mai pushed me aside. "Like that's going to help him understand." Then she spoke quickly to Kasem in Thai. It was good to see she was back to her old annoying self. Kasem nodded again and pointed to one of the taller resort buildings a short distance away. "This way."

So we followed him into the broken city of Patong Beach.

The three of us hurried as fast as we could. But it was hard going. We had to climb over toppled trees, broken pavement and pieces of cement.

It was eerie how few people were in the streets, or what was left of the streets. That is, how many living people there were. Mostly there were bodies. Every now and then an arm or a leg would stick out from a piece of pavement or broken junk. Someone one could still be alive. But if we didn't keep moving fast we'd be down there with them. So we didn't stop. We just kept moving toward the resort.

When we reached the hotel, my heart sank. Sure, it was tall enough to be able to get above the next wave. And I was pretty sure that it would survive the second one since it had stood up to the first one.

But the first two floors were so damaged that there was no way for us to get in.

"This just keeps getting worse," I said. I pounded my fist against a car that had rammed into the hotel. I turned to Mai and Kasem and suddenly felt very, very tired.

"Luke, are you okay?" Mai asked.

What now? We had to do something, and fast. The wave was almost at the shore. "Any ideas?"

Kasem, to my surprise, took charge. He slapped me on the back and said, "We climb, man." He pointed to a fifth-floor balcony above us.

I realized what he had in mind and nodded. This just might work. The balconies on the third floor were in pretty bad shape. But there was one on the

fifth floor close to the building's corner. There were designs carved into the bricks that ran all the way up each corner. It wasn't my idea of great art, but they might make decent footholds. It wouldn't be an easy climb. Still, it was better than getting washed away by a giant wave.

"You okay with climbing that?" I asked Mai.

I was in for another surprise. Mai might be afraid of water, but heights were easy for her. "Are you kidding? Just like rock-wall climbing, right?" Then she started to climb like a monkey going up a tree.

Kasem followed behind her.

It was slower for me. I wasn't about to admit it to Mai, but I really don't like heights. My arms were still stinging from hauling Mai and Kasem out of the water. My back and neck ached from my jump onto the overpass. My fingers were already bleeding. And I've got a lot more weight to sling up.

But I looked out to the beach and saw that the wave was already there. It was getting ready to swallow Patong Beach again.

So I climbed. I was breathing hard by the time I was halfway up.

Then I got clumsy.

I grabbed hold of a stone just as my right foot slipped. I spent a terrifying minute dangling by my fingertips. My feet kept swinging, trying to get a foothold again. Blood was running freely down my hands and wrists.

"Luke, get a grip and get up here!" Mai yelled from the balcony. She and Kasem had already reached the fifth floor. "It's coming!"

"What do you think I'm trying to do?" I muttered. Then my foot finally found a spot. I steadied myself and started to climb again. I winced with every move. My hands were raw and scraped. My stomach was doing flips because I was up so high.

Finally, I hauled myself up and over the balcony wall. I fell to the floor just as the wave hit.

Kasem was right to choose the fifth floor. The wave almost made it to the fourth. And this time it carried even more destruction with it. There was broken glass from shattered windows, cars, boats, trucks. And bodies. So many more bodies.

I wanted to curl up like a baby and cry. It was all too much. I jumped as Kasem put his hand on my shoulder.

"We must go inside, man," he said. Then he picked

up a metal chair and smashed it through the window.

We climbed through the broken window and into the hotel room. Mai seemed to be okay, but all I could do was collapse on the floor.

We were safe for the moment. But for how long?

Chapter 5
Food and Water

For hours, all I could think of was getting away from the wave. We had made it. We were alive and had made it to somewhere safe. But now that we were in a dry room, high up from the water, a different problem showed its ugly face.

Where was Mom? Was she safe? And then, of course, the most terrible question. Was she alive?

I should have slept. Lord knows, I was exhausted. But worry is a terrible thing. It curls up in your gut and gnaws at your insides.

I needed to do something. But what? I got up and paced the room.

It took me a few minutes to realize that Mai wasn't

beside me. She'd gone into the bathroom a good twenty minutes ago.

I walked to the bathroom door and put my ear against it. I could hear Mai sobbing quietly, like she was trying to keep it secret.

"Mai, are you okay?" I called through the door. A stupid question, but still I asked it.

"Go away, Luke," she replied.

Then I realized that Mai must be just as worried as I was.

Of course, Mai wouldn't be worried about *my* mother. It was her dad that she cared about. It was her dad that had brought my mom to Patong Beach. They'd met online and somehow hit it off. Now I was supposed to meet this great guy from Thailand. I was supposed to give them my blessing to get married and then have a great week on the beach. It was going to be the best vacation ever.

Yeah, right.

"Mai, maybe your dad is okay. I mean, we made it through this. He's older and smarter than both of us. Don't you think he could be all right too?"

Mai came flying out of the bathroom. Her face was red and puffy from crying. She waved her arms and yelled, "What do you care? You really hate my father. I bet you'd be happy if he was dead. Wouldn't that solve all your problems, Luke? Wouldn't it?"

If she had stabbed me straight through the heart, it couldn't have hurt more. Sure, I didn't want her dad to marry my mom. But wish him dead? After all the death we'd seen? How could Mai even think that?

It all came crashing over me. The worry about my mom. Mai accusing me of things she knew nothing about. Images of bodies littering the streets. The monster wave trying to pull me under. They all swirled around in my brain. That's when I lost it.

"You selfish little brat!" I yelled. "Don't you think I'm worried too? My mom is out there somewhere. And I don't even know if she's. . . ." I couldn't finish the sentence. I just stood there, glaring at her.

Kasem stepped between us. "Don't fight, guys." He put his hand on my shoulder and searched for the English words. "No time to fight. We need food. Clothes. Let's go look."

I took deep breaths to get the anger under control. My fists clenched and unclenched. I could feel the heat wash through me.

Kasem grabbed both my shoulders and made me

face him. He waited until I was calm enough to make eye contact. "Soon there's no lights. No radio. It's day now. We need food, water. We need to look now." Then he said something to Mai in Thai.

Mai wiped her eyes and took a deep breath. She didn't look at me when she spoke. "He's right, Luke. We have to find food and water and anything else we might need. There's no power and we don't know how long it's going to be out. It's going to get really dark when night falls."

Mai didn't speak to me again the rest of that day. We split up. She took off with Kasem to find clothing, and, if we were lucky, a flashlight and a radio. I was in charge of finding food and water.

The first thing Kasem had done was to take a rolling suitcase from the closet. He emptied its contents on the floor. "Put food and water in here," he said to me. Then he took off with Mai and I was on my own.

Kasem's words made sense. It was easier for me to lug a suitcase from room to room than to keep coming back with armloads of stuff.

But it wasn't *my stuff*. The suitcase, the food, the

bottled water; it all belonged to someone else. I'm not perfect. But I'm not a thief either. And this sure felt like stealing.

I struggled with the whole idea of it. Then I made a decision. I took a pen and pad of paper from the desk in our room. As I traveled from room to empty room, I left an IOU that included my name and email. At the end of each I wrote, *Sorry for taking this. Hope you understand. Will pay you back.*

It would have been easier to go through the halls, but room doors were locked. So I had to climb from balcony to balcony on the outside of the building. I'd check each room to see if the patio doors were locked. Luckily for me, many people had left in a hurry. Most of the doors were left open.

I tried not to think about how high up I was as I climbed to the next balcony. Or about all the destruction and death below me.

Food and water, Luke, I kept saying to myself. *Focus on that.* And try not to think about what might have happened to my mom.

Chapter 6 The Dark

The rooms were strangely quiet. The only light was what spilled through a window here and there. It was spooky moving through all that darkness, so I talked to myself to give myself courage.

"Tofu?" I said as I pulled a paper bag from a dresser drawer. "Who brings tofu on vacation?" But I put it into my bag. "Mai might want it." I couldn't believe that I'd ever be *that* hungry.

I cleared out all the bottled water and juice I could put my hands on. Food was harder to find, so I had to settle for chips, peanuts and chocolate bars. Once in a while, I found a granola bar or bag of dried fruit. My stomach growled. I hadn't eaten since breakfast. But I stopped myself from eating any of it now. We had no idea how long we'd be without power. There were no working TVs, radios or phones. And we didn't know if another wave would hit or how much damage the last two had done.

All the while, I tried as hard as I could to keep the other thoughts out of my head.

And I failed.

Images of bodies, wide-eyed and bloated, kept flashing through my mind. My mother's eyes, hurt and angry as she ordered me to stay in our room this morning. This morning. . . . Was it really only that morning when we'd fought? It seemed like a long time ago.

"I'm sorry, Mom," I said in the dark room. I was talking to myself of course, but it felt good. Quietly I added, "And please don't be dead."

Then I understood why Mai had locked herself in the bathroom to cry. The pain I felt was too much for anyone else to see. I sat on the rumpled bed of the hotel room and let the despair wash over me.

"Please. Please. Please!" I'm not sure who I was begging to let my mom be okay. But I knew that there was nothing I wouldn't do to make things okay again.

"Just let me find her," I pleaded. "Let me tell her I'm sorry. She can marry Mai's father if that's going to make her happy. Just let her be okay." Then I buried my head in my hands.

I'm not sure how long they stood there in the open patio doorway. I heard Kasem clear his throat. "Dark soon, man. We'll stay here now."

I guess Mai and Kasem saw me climb into the room and followed me as far as the balcony door. There weren't many more rooms for us to search on this floor. As I looked out the window, I realized that Kasem was right. We'd been searching through rooms for over an hour. The sun was now low on the horizon. It would be dark soon.

I took a few deep breaths to steady myself. "Yeah, sounds like a plan."

Mai came to sit beside me. Her face was hidden behind her long black hair. "I was mad at you," she whispered. "I didn't mean what I said."

"Me neither," I answered. "I kind of lost it back there. I think my nerves are pretty raw."

Mai seemed to understand. She nodded and patted my shoulder. "Let's sort what we found before it gets too dark."

We spent the next half-hour sorting food and water and dividing up clothes. Mai and Kasem had found one flashlight, a compass and a few batteries. We'd have to use them sparingly. The flashlight would barely last through the night. We chose to save the batteries just in case. That meant we had to spend the night in the dark.

City people don't realize how much light we take

for granted. That night in Patong Beach, not one street light, not one lamp or nightlight shone. It was pitch black. The only sounds we heard were the chilling noise of water moving in the town. And above that, were the wails of survivors mourning their dead.

Mai, Kasem and I shared an odd meal there in the dark. Just as I thought, Mai thought the tofu was a real treasure. I guess there's no accounting for taste. I ate a granola bar and bag of trail mix and washed it down with some orange juice.

As we ate, Kasem tried to talk with me. He started out in his careful English, but it was hard for me to understand. He quickly gave up and spoke in Thai. Mai translated for him. I'd answer and she'd translate back again. I realized then that having Mai and Kasem with me during this crisis was a godsend. Mai spoke the language and Kasem knew the city.

"We met a couple of tourists in room 562," Mai translated. It was an odd feeling. I could hear Mai's voice, but I couldn't see her in the darkness. "There's lots of talk going on right now. People were worried about a third wave that was supposed to hit. Some said it would come at one o'clock, some said two. When that one didn't come, they said three o'clock. They made the third wave sound like it was news from the government, so everyone was afraid."

"That makes sense," I said.

"There were two tourists hiding out up here like us," Mai went on, "but they went off to a hill on the outskirts of town. They say there's high ground that the waves can't reach. Maybe we should do the same."

"No way!" I shook my head firmly. "I'm going to look for my mom." I'd already made the decision even before we sat in the pitch black room.

Mai was silent for a moment. She didn't need to translate my answer for Kasem. He started talking in Thai. Mai shushed him with one stern word.

"Do you have any kind of plan?" she asked.

That kind of stopped me. I had a plan, but it was pretty rough. I wasn't even sure I could explain it.

"Well, we know my mom and your dad were going to meet your family at a restaurant. You remember. . . ." I tried hard to remember the restaurant's name, but it was lost in the fog of my mind.

Mai started talking quickly in Thai to Kasem. I realized that she was asking about the restaurant.

"Yes, I think I know this place," Kasem said in English. "Not far, man. But hard to get there. Patong is so . . . broken".

I knew what he meant. The city was "broken". Finding our way over cars, boats and building rubble would be tough. The roads were in pieces or covered in mud. "But I *could* get there, right?"

"Yes, man. Would take two, three hours, maybe."

"What if you get there to find it's destroyed?" Mai voiced the fear I hadn't been able to speak.

"It's a chance I'll have to take," I answered. "At least I've got somewhere to start looking." I searched for the right words before I told Mai what I needed to say. "Mai, tomorrow I'm going to go looking for my mom. I'll go with or without you. But I'd really like you to come along." I swallowed my pride and went on. "You'd be real helpful to translate . . . if I need to ask people about my mom."

"And my dad?" she asked.

"Of course we'd look for him too. They were together when they left. They're probably still together, don't you think?"

"Of course they're together." Then Mai surprised me again by adding. "Dad loves your mom, you know. He'd never let anything happen to her."

"Good," Kasem's voice broke in. Then he yawned

loudly. "Let's sleep now. We'll look in the morning."

I curled up on one of the hotel room's double beds, but it was hard to sleep. I thought about how selfish Mai and I had been. Mom and Mai's dad loved each other. Who were we to steal that happiness away from them? Who were we to stand in the way of their marriage?

You'll get the chance to tell Mom when you see her, I said to myself.

But what if you don't get the chance to say you're sorry?

I tried to lock out that nagging inner voice.

Then I fell into a fitful sleep.

Chapter 7

The Search

Morning light spilled through the hotel window. At first, I wasn't sure what woke me. Then I understood: it was the silence. It was really weird. The streets that were busy with cars and tourists only yesterday were empty now. Empty and silent.

It was hot and sweaty in the room. For breakfast, we ate only enough to take the edge off our hunger.

"You carry the food, Luke," Kasem ordered as he loaded most of it into a small backpack. He only put a small amount into his pack and Mai's. "You're big, strong. You can protect it."

I stood there with my mouth hanging open as I realized what he meant. "You don't think it's really come to that, Kasem?" I couldn't believe that people would try to steal food from us. How could anyone do something like that?

Kasem looked at me with sad, tired eyes. "There are good people in Patong Beach," he said. "But bad people, too. Just stay careful. Watch with your eyes."

I still didn't want to believe it. But I took Kasem's advice. I strapped the bag tightly over my shoulders.

As we climbed slowly down from the balcony and onto the street, two things hit me like a slap in the face.

The awful heat.

And the smell.

The town smelled like a garbage heap, only worse. It smelled of things dead and rotting.

Something ran across Mai's foot and she screamed. A rat. But not just one rat, hundreds of them. The rats that managed to escape the tsunami were now out in the streets. My stomach lurched when I realized what they were doing. The rats were feeding on the dead bodies. They were joined by the insects that buzzed all around us.

I almost lost my nerve and darted back to the safety of the hotel. Then I thought about my mom out there.

I firmed my shoulders and turned to Mai. "If this is going to be too hard for you, I'll understand. I can ask Kasem to take you to the hill with the others."

"No way," Mai answered, though I could tell she was shaking. "My dad's out there, too. I'm going with you."

So Kasem led the way. The three of us headed out to find the restaurant where Mom and Mai's dad had been.

We climbed over scrap heaps, broken concrete, toppled cars and trees. Kasem tried his best to keep clear of the bodies. But it was tough going. The wave had washed bodies up everywhere. Not just human bodies; there were dogs too. Lots of them.

Thailand is known for its dogs. Mostly they run loose in packs in the streets. The Thai people feed them and let them roam freely. Now the streets of Patong had no four-legged beggars. They'd been pulled under when the wave hit.

We saw rescue workers in some spots. They were joined by locals who had survived the two big waves. I wanted so much to stop and help. But each minute I delayed was a minute further away from finding my mom.

My legs and arms ached after an hour. Then it took another hour until we reached the spot where the restaurant should have been.

"No, no, no!" Mai cried out.

There was no restaurant in front of us. The building had been destroyed by the wave. There was only a pile of broken brick and smashed glass.

A frustrated scream started inside me, but got caught in my throat. I couldn't believe what I saw. I ran to the wreckage and started to search. Kasem tried to pull me back, but I shook him off.

I pulled away pieces of broken wood and brick, bits of chairs and tables. An old man started to yell at me in Thai. He waved his arms wildly.

I turned to him with angry eyes.

"Stop, Luke." Kasem put his hand gently on my shoulder. He switched to Thai and spoke quickly to Mai.

She translated for me. "This man used to own the restaurant . . . what's left of it, I mean." Mai forced me to look at her. "There's nothing here."

"So what's his problem?" I asked.

"Looters have already been in the streets. So he thinks you're trying to steal from him."

"Ask him if he knows anything about my mom and your dad," I said. But Mai was already speaking to the old man in Thai.

Mai had tears in her eyes when she turned back to me. "He remembers them, Luke. He says they got out before the big wave hit. The last time he saw them, they were running with the crowds."

"Does he know where they went?" My heart was racing.

Mai asked, but shook her head. "He says there was too much chaos. But he thinks we should try a hotel at the edge of town. He heard that they're setting up a place where people can put up pictures of people who are lost." Mai swallowed hard. "He thinks we might find them there." Mai spoke to the man a little more and got directions.

For the first time since yesterday's tragedy, I felt a stirring of hope.

Would I find Mom there?

That nagging voice piped in to taunt me.

Yes, but will you find her alive?

The trek to the hotel should have been faster. But we were slowed down by all the junk we had to climb over. And we stopped now and then when we met someone along the way. They were just like us – searching for friends and loved ones. Mai would ask them if they'd seen our parents. They would pull out pictures of the ones they'd lost and ask if we'd seen them. It was such a sad way to meet. I felt bad that I didn't even have a picture of my mom with me.

One tourist stopped me. "Do you have any food? I haven't eaten since yesterday."

I opened my pack and offered him a granola bar.

Kasem grabbed my arm and pulled me aside. "No, Luke."

"Don't worry," I answered. "I'll take it from my ration. You don't expect me to let this guy go hungry, do you?"

Kasem shook his head and muttered. I'd been around Mai long enough to know that he was swearing in Thai.

As we moved along the block, we came across a group of men and women who were digging in the rubble. I could see that they'd already pulled out a number of bodies. They'd lined them up and covered them with blankets.

A local woman grabbed my arm and pleaded, "Help us. My husband, my little girl . . . they were in there." She pointed to a building where the main floor had collapsed. People were trying to pull away concrete and wood to get inside.

Every bit of me wanted to say no, to keep searching for Mom. But I looked into the woman's eyes and knew that she was about the same age as my mother. Was Mom doing the same thing? Begging people to help find her son? If Mom were here, what would she do? So I only had one choice.

"Wait up," I called out to Mai and Kasem. "These people need help."

Mai started to argue, then she looked into my eyes and stopped. "Luke, it will slow us down."

"Let's say we do find Mom and your dad." I grabbed Mai by the shoulders. "Do you want to tell them that we let people die instead of helping them?"

"But these people. . . ." Mai came close and whispered. "Look at the building, Luke. Do you think that anyone in there would still be alive?"

"I have to believe that, Mai." I tried to make her understand. "If we can help, and if there is someone alive, then maybe. . . ." My voice got caught in my throat. I swallowed hard. "Then maybe my mom and your dad are alive too."

Mai hung her head for a moment. Then she looked me in the eyes. "Okay, Luke. Just this once. Tell us what you want us to do."

It was horrible work. The smell. The bodies. My hands started bleeding again as we pulled away broken wood and stone. I closed my mind to someone crying as another body was pulled from the ruins.

"Kasem, help me with this," I called. I was pulling on one large beam of wood.

It took us a couple of tries, but we managed to free it. That's when I heard some voices inside the ruins. The voices were faint, but human.

"What are they saying?" I asked Kasem.

"No words, man. Just happy we're here."

Chapter 8 Found and Lost

"Over here!" I yelled to the others. They all came rushing in, and we started to dig that much harder.

It was slow work pulling the rest of the rubble away. We had to be careful that the rest of the building didn't come crashing down. But we made slow progress. The voices inside became louder . . . closer to us. Then we could see an arm, a face and a hand. And finally, we pulled them to safety.

An old gray-haired couple came out first. They had to shield their eyes from the sun. "Thank you, thank you," they kept saying. After them came a man and a little girl. Rushing to them was the woman who had asked me to help. She hugged her husband and daughter. Then she turned and hugged me. I thought she was going to squeeze all the air out of me.

She kept on saying something like "*korp kun,*" over and over. Now I don't know much Thai, but I know she meant "thank you," and that came from deep in her heart.

As I watched the family together, a warm feeling spread through me. I imagined seeing my own mom again. I imagined a world without all this loss and pain.

Then I heard another sound. It was faint. And it was coming from under the rubble. I put my ear to the caved-in wall and listened harder. "Is that what I think it is?"

I pulled a few more boards away. In the darkness below, I saw a pair of yellow eyes.

The dog was too far down to climb up and out of the hole we'd made.

"Kasem, come help me," I called.

While Kasem held my ankles, I lowered half my body inside the hole. I held a flashlight with my teeth so that I could see. It took a few tries, but I got the dog to come closer. He seemed to understand and took a leap up so I could grab him. In minutes, Kasem was

dragging us both from the hole.

"He doesn't have a collar," Mai said.

The dog was skinny and dirty, but he didn't seem hurt. He gave a little yelp and then whimpered.

Kasem just laughed at him. "A beggar dog, this one." Then Kasem thumped me on the back. "Let's go now, man. This day is gone soon."

I could see that the sun was already high in the sky.

We'd been digging for hours. If we didn't get going soon, we wouldn't have enough daylight left to reach the hotel.

I got a few more hugs from the people we'd pulled out of the building. My face was red and I had a big lump in my throat when we said goodbye.

Then we headed out.

"Luke, I think you have a fan." Mai laughed, maybe her first laugh since the wave hit.

The little dog was close at my heels. If I walked, he walked. If I stopped, he stopped. "Shoo," I said. "Go home."

Kasem broke in, "He has no home, Luke. This dog's homeless." He patted the dog's head.

"Well, he can't come with us. We've got enough to worry about with just us three." I shooed the dog one more time.

I should have saved my breath. No matter what I did, the dog followed me.

So I gave up. Now the four of us made our way across the broken town. Soon, we came to a street that was completely blocked with toppled trees and broken cars.

"We should go this way, man." Kasem led us into

an old building. He explained more in Thai to Mai.

"Kasem says we should be able to find our way to the next street if we go through the building." Mai frowned. "It's going to be dark in there. But I don't see what other choice we have."

I took out our flashlight and prayed that the batteries would last. Then we entered the dark, narrow hallways. I led the way with Mai and Kasem close behind. The dog held back. I guess being trapped in one building was enough for him. *Good,* I thought, *maybe that dumb dog will leave me alone now.*

We walked carefully. The wave had washed branches and broken furniture into parts of the hallways. When we were deep inside the building, a sound made me stop in my tracks.

Click, scratch, click. Someone was scraping something against the brick walls. Then I heard laughter. It wasn't the kind of laughter that made you want to smile. It was the kind that made you want to run for your life. And it was directly ahead of us.

"Go back," I whispered to Mai and Kasem.

But it was too late. The gang must have seen us go into the building because they came from behind us and in front of us.

"Not so fast, friend." It was the leader who spoke to us. He said *friend* but made it sound like an insult. "I'll take those backpacks to start with. And all you have in your pockets." His knife shone in the glow from my flashlight.

The gang must have seen me give food to that tourist and been waiting for the chance to get us alone. I wanted to kick myself for being so stupid.

Another thug pulled Mai into the light. He ripped off the gold pendant Mai always wore around her neck. "Hey, Boss Man," he yelled to the leader. "What kind of rich daddy buys his girl something like this?"

I was ready to put up a fight. I started to move at the leader, my fists raised. But the rest of the gang hit me from behind. Before I knew it, I was knocked hard to the ground. I could hear Kasem shout and Mai scream. Then the backpack was ripped from my hands.

"Leave us alone!" I yelled and tried to get to my feet.

The leader jumped on me and raised his knife. "You don't give orders, friend."

That's when it all got crazy.

There was a loud growl and the dog leapt over

me and onto the leader. It snarled and snapped and wrestled him to the ground.

The gang's leader fell off me. Then he cursed and held his arm where the dog bit him. He yelled something in Thai and the gang fled back into the darkness.

The dog's wet nose bumped against my face. Then he licked me and barked. He must have known he had done a good job.

"Yeah, yeah. Thanks," I said and patted his head.

I picked up the flashlight that had rolled away. That's when I saw Kasem, who was lying a few feet away.

"You okay?" I went to see if he was injured. He seemed just fine.

I panned the area with my light. "Mai," I called, "you all right, Mai?"

No one answered.

The hairs at the back of my neck stood on end. "MAI!" Her named bounced off the dark walls.

That's when I realized that the gang had taken more than our food.

They'd taken Mai.

Chapter 9 A Battle

I was frantic. Why would the gang take Mai? My mind tried to come up with some reasons. *Would they hurt her? Will they kill her?* The thoughts that ripped through my brain made my skin crawl.

"This is my fault," I said to Kasem. I paced back and forth in the rubble-lined street. "I was supposed to look after Mai. It's all my fault!"

Kasem could only understand half of what I was saying. He shook his head and then thumped me hard on the back. "Don't panic, man. Let's get help."

"But where would they take Mai? How will we find her?" I guess all of the stress of the last two days was finally catching up with me. I couldn't think straight.

Kasem grabbed hold of my arm and squeezed until it hurt. "Let's get help *now,* Luke!" Then he gave me a rough shove. "Follow me."

The dog came close to me and growled a warning at Kasem. I guess in his dog brain he was my protector.

I followed Kasem through broken streets. The dog kept close to my side. My mind was numb by the time we'd retraced our steps. We went back to where we'd rescued the family an hour ago.

The searchers were still there, helping to pull more bodies from the rubble. They covered them up to restore some sort of dignity. I watched the flies buzz in the hot air above the growing pile of corpses. It made my stomach churn. Was that how we'd find Mai?

Kasem took charge. He went to the searchers and spoke in excited Thai. The woman whose husband and daughter we'd saved came over to me. She could speak English. "Don't you worry, Luke. You helped us. Now it's our turn to help you. We'll find your sister."

I almost told her that Mai wasn't my sister. She was my not-quite stepsister. But I had to stop myself. Something had changed between me and Mai since the tsunami. My mom and her dad weren't married yet. But Mai sure felt like a sister to me now. *Will she ever get a chance to be one?* I wondered.

"Why would the gang kidnap Mai?" I dreaded the answer. But I had to ask.

The woman paused, like she was searching for the right words. "You have to understand . . . Thailand has many good people in it," she told me. "But there are bad people here too. They saw from Mai's clothes and jewelry that she comes from a rich family."

"What do you mean?" Rage boiled inside me.

The woman sighed. "They're betting your family will pay lots of money to get her back." She hugged me again. "But don't you worry, Luke, we'll find her. We'll get her back soon."

"But what if they . . . hurt Mai?" I couldn't say the word *kill*. It was just too horrible to think about.

"They wouldn't be that stupid, Luke. She's worth too much alive. Besides, we've heard rumors about this gang. We may know where they've taken her." She patted my hand and then called to the others.

There were only eight of us when we started down the street. But every time we passed someone, the woman would stop. She'd explain what we were doing, and half of them would join us. That's when I realized that she was right. There were many good people in Thailand. By the time we reached the old warehouse where the gang hung out, we had a small crowd. We'd picked up pieces of two-by-four and tire irons, anything we could find that could be used as a weapon.

"In there?" I asked, pointing at the warehouse. It was a big building, not much damaged by the flooding water.

"Maybe," Kasem said. "If it's the right gang . . . and they're still inside."

"Will they fight us?"

"They think your sister is worth big money," Kasem said. "Of course they will fight. But all of us will fight harder." He smiled and lifted up a tire iron.

It was time to go in. I pushed my way in with the rest of our group. The warehouse had a small fire pit in the middle to light it. Otherwise it was cold and dark.

The gang had heard us. In no time, one of the gang was coming at me. I whacked him with a broken ship's mast. The dog was beside me, snapping and snarling. In truth, I think he scared the guy more than I did.

Then more gang members came out. Some had

knives, some just pieces of wood. But they weren't as tough as they looked. I jumped at them, shouting like a madman. The dog came with me, snarling like a wolf. Soon our crowd of volunteers sent them running. Then we got back to searching through the building.

"Mai!" I shouted.

"Luke, in here!" Mai's voice was faint.

"Where?" I shouted back. But something hard struck me behind the knees and I tumbled to the floor.

"YOU!" The gang leader pinned me down with his knees. "I think we finish it this time, eh, friend?"

I've never been much of a fighter. But then again, I've never had much to fight for. Every bit of rage and worry from the past two days rushed up inside me. I put all my weight into pushing the guy. He wasn't expecting it and toppled backward.

That's when my dog defender came to stand beside me. We must have looked quite a sight. Me, red and angry like a bull. The dog with his ears flat against his head, his fur standing on end and his teeth bared. The gang leader took one look at us and bolted for safety. The rest of his gang wasn't far behind him.

We found Mai and three other young girls locked in a small room. They looked dirty and afraid, but otherwise okay. With them were piles of supplies. Food, water, clothing, cigarettes and liquor were piled in corners.

I untied Mai's hands and feet and gave her a hug. "You okay?" I asked.

"I am now," she said with just the hint of a smile.

Chapter 10 Wall of the Lost

We filled our backpacks again with food and water. I was careful to only take what we already had in our packs. It didn't seem right to take food the gang had stolen from other people. Fair is fair, even in a disaster.

As we got ready to leave, I couldn't thank the people enough. They had all been strangers and yet they'd risked their lives to save Mai. I guess a disaster can bring the best out in people.

I made sure that Mai was okay after what she'd been through. Mai said she was, so the three of us headed out onto the streets.

This time, when the dog trotted beside me, I didn't complain.

"He needs a name," Mai said as she patted the dog's head. "How about Champ?"

Since he'd scared off the gang, Champ seemed like as good a name as any.

"Okay, Champ," I said to him. "You're one of us now. Maybe you can help find my mom."

"And my dad," Mai added.

I just smiled. We were looking for our lost family, simple as that.

We'd tied some cloths around our faces to block the smell. They worked well. But the bugs were something else. They buzzed around our heads like crazy. When we saw them swarming near the ground, we did our best to steer clear. That could only mean one thing. Something dead was lying there.

It took an hour to make our way through the streets of Patong Beach. Rescue workers were going through the streets, too. The dead had to be taken away. The injured needed help. Even those of us who had survived were like walking wounded.

When we made it to the gathering place, I couldn't believe what I saw. A huge wall, covered with photos and hand-written notes stood before us. It was surrounded by hundreds of people looking at the

photographs. They were all trying to find loved ones lost in the tsunami. Every few minutes someone would stop us to ask in Thai or English, "Have you seen this person?"

So many missing. So many lost. So many dead. My mind was numb from the idea of it.

At the wall, we heard some news from the outside world. The tsunami hadn't just hit us. It had flooded fourteen countries along the Indian Ocean. We heard many different counts of how many people were dead or missing. The truth was, no one really knew. Too many people were just washed out with the wave. No one knew if their bodies would ever be found.

I kept trying to describe my mom to the people I met. But it was very hard. I felt bad that I couldn't remember what Mom had been wearing that last day. I just remembered her angry face glaring at me. A lousy memory.

Still, I kept asking for help. Again and again, I'd stop people and ask. "My mother, have you seen my mother?"

But no one remembered seeing her.

Then Mai's voice called to me, "Luke, over here!"

I ran through the crowd. Mai was looking up at a photo on the wall. It was my Grade 10 school photo. I hated that photo, but I knew Mom kept it with her.

Under the photo, Mom had written *PLEASE, have you seen my son?* It went on to describe me and Mai, and that I was traveling with her. Beneath it was the name of a hotel. Kasem said that hotel was way inland and up on higher ground.

My heart raced. Now I knew where to find her.

I turned to Mai with a big grin on my face. But my smile died quickly. Mai was still searching the board and muttering in Thai. The sun was starting to fade, so much of the wall was in shadow. Still, Mai squinted and kept searching. That's when it hit me – my mom's note had said nothing about Mai's father.

At last, Mai crumpled to her knees and started to cry.

I crouched beside her and tried to put my arm around her. Mai just pushed me away. "He's gone."

"We don't know that, Mai," I tried to tell her.

"You don't understand. He would have left a note." Mai sniffed and wiped her eyes. "He wouldn't let your mom leave a message and not leave one for me too. He'd know we would stop here to check." Mai rocked with her arms wrapped around her knees. "He's gone," she repeated. Then she buried her face in her hands.

I felt sorry for Mai, and I feared that she was right. Of course, I wanted to press on, to make it to the hotel where my mom would be waiting. Maybe we would find Mai's dad there with her. But the logical part of my brain said that Mai was right. Mai's dad would have left a note. Why didn't he?

I tried to urge Mai to get up and get going. She

shrugged me away.

"We can't stay here," I said as gently as I could.

"No, I'm not moving," Mai said firmly. "My dad's gone. What's the point of searching any more?"

Kasem had been standing to the side watching us. He piped in, "Better to stay here now, Luke. Dark soon anyway."

I looked to the horizon and gave a sigh. Night was falling quickly on Patong Beach. There was still no hydro for lights. And it was too dangerous to move in the dark. We'd have to wait until morning.

Kasem and I took turns trying to comfort Mai. But it was like she'd built a giant wall around herself. She just sat and stared into the growing darkness.

Kasem and I spent that night listening to people tell stories about how the wave had hit them. They spoke of the horror of watching their loved ones get snatched away by the water. Some shared news they'd heard about other places and countries. There were so many rumors and stories going around. It was hard to tell what was truth and what was gossip.

As the night wore on, I curled up to Champ's warm, flea-bitten body. I wondered what it would be like when I saw my mother again. I tried to come up with the words I would say to her. But at least I knew that Mom was alive.

A few feet away, Mai cried herself into a fitful sleep. Her dad was certainly among the lost. He might well be among the dead.

Chapter 11 Have You Seen My Mom?

We left at the first light of dawn. Mai walked like a zombie beside us. Even Champ seemed to pick up on her sadness. He padded along quietly with his head down and his tail tucked between his legs.

The inland hotel was a hive of action. It reminded me of the images I'd seen of refugee camps on the news. There were lineups of people, all looking tired and dirty. A makeshift hospital was set up and had spilled out into the parking lot and street. Injured people were sitting and lying all over. Other people lined up for food and water. Some just looked like they were lost, still in shock from the events of the past two days.

"How are we going to find my mom in all this?" I said to Mai. "I think it would be best if we split up. We can cover more ground that way."

Mai seemed to stare right through me. But she answered quietly, "Sure, Luke. Just tell me what to do."

Mai was really starting to worry me. It wasn't like Mai to be so quiet. Or so agreeable.

"Kasem, will you stay with Mai?" There was no point in Kasem searching on his own. He didn't know what my mom looked like. And I didn't like the idea of Mai being alone after what she'd been through.

Kasem thumped me on the back. "Sure, Luke. We meet back here in . . . two hours." Then he put his arm around Mai's shoulders and guided her through the crowd.

I felt bad watching them walk away. But I couldn't wait any longer. I had to find Mom!

I forced my way into the sea of people around the hotel. There were so many faces. Now and then I'd see a woman with light brown hair and I'd run to her, only to find that it wasn't Mom. "Sorry," I kept saying. I was met with tears or blank eyes still filled with shock.

People stopped me, too. They were on the same mission as I was. Had I seen their son or daughter?

One woman grabbed my hand. "My little girl," she cried. "I was holding her . . . but the wave . . . it was so strong. She was in my arms. Then she was gone."

A man shoved a picture in my face. "My wife. Have you seen my wife?"

An old woman pleaded, "Where are the doctors? My husband needs a doctor."

Their voices flew around in my brain until it felt like it would explode.

I raced from person to person, trying so hard to describe my mother to them. But they'd just shake their heads and suggest that I look somewhere else. If only I had a picture . . . or something.

So many times, I'd be sure I saw her and my heart would lift. I'd push my way through the crowd. But it would just be another tourist. Another lost soul.

I wanted to scream. She had to be here!

A kind man put his hand on my shoulder. "Have you looked inside the hotel, son? They keep people who are badly hurt in there, I think."

"But she's not hurt," I explained. "We just got separated."

He looked at me with sad eyes. I could see that he thought I was being too hopeful. Then, he looked

around at all the damage and shook his head. “Good luck, then,” was all he said before he walked away.

I turned to look at the big glass doors that led into the hotel. “Stay here, Champ,” I ordered. I could tell that my dog wanted nothing more than to follow me into the building. But he did as he was told. For once.

The hotel lobby felt cool compared with the heat outside. There still wasn't any power so it was dark, only lit with candles or oil lamps. I could tell it had been turned into a hospital without even seeing. The smell struck me as soon as I walked in.

People moaned on cots and blankets on the floor. I picked my way through the hallways. Then I made it into what would have been their main meeting room. Now it was a maze of makeshift beds.

As my eyes adjusted to the dark room, I looked from corner to corner.

Then I saw her.

My mother was bent over the body of a man.

And she was crying.

Chapter 12

Reunion

For a moment, I was frozen in the doorway of the hotel's makeshift hospital room. For two days, I'd been searching for Mom. I'd survived two killer waves, saved Mai from drowning and ridden a runaway bus through raging waters. I'd scaled the side of a building, rescued survivors and gotten jumped by thieves. Now, at last, I'd found my mother.

And I couldn't move.

I remembered how mean I'd been to Mom yesterday morning. I could still see the angry, disappointed face before she slammed the door and left.

Now I watched my mother hunched over, crying her heart out.

What could I say to her?

Then she looked up. Her eyes got very wide. Mom screamed my name so loud that everyone turned to look.

I almost flew through the room. I leapt over people until I reached the corner where Mom stood waiting. I didn't care who was looking. I hugged her as tightly as I could.

"I'm sorry, Mom," I repeated over and over. "I'm so sorry."

I couldn't hear her answer. All the people around us were clapping and cheering.

Mom was crying again. But this time, they were happy tears. "Where were you? Where's Mai? Are you hurt?" The words rushed out of her.

"Mai's outside looking for you. We split up when we got here." I started to tell Mom about all we'd been through.

Then I heard from across the room. "Hey, Luke!" Kasem must have heard the noise from outside. He stood in the doorway with Mai at his side.

Mom covered her mouth and started to cry again. "I was so afraid that we'd lost the two of you." She waved for Mai to join us.

Mai started out slowly. She moved carefully around the people who were lying and sitting on the beds.

Then Mai noticed the man lying at Mom's feet.

"Dad!" Mai rushed to her father's side. "What happened to him? Is he okay?"

"He's just sleeping," Mom explained. "Don't worry. The doctors say he broke some ribs. They gave him some strong painkillers that knocked him out." She gave Mai a bear hug. "He was so worried about you, Mai. So was I. What happened to you?"

It took awhile to tell Mom how we'd survived the past two days. Mai filled in the gaps as I told our story. Three days ago, if Mai interrupted me, it made me mad. Now, it just made me smile.

And Mai was her real self again. All the worry was lifted from her face.

Kasem joined the three of us. Mai translated for him. He'd add to our story and Mai would explain what he'd said.

When none of us had any words left, Mom sat with her head leaning against my shoulder. Mai sat holding her father's hand. Kasem went to make sure that Champ had some food and water.

I was dead tired. I'd barely slept for two days, but I

couldn't rest. There was something that I still needed to do.

"Mom . . ." I began.

Mom straightened up and looked me in the eye. "Yes?"

"I've had a lot of time to think about how selfish I've been. . . ."

Mom started to tell me that everything was okay. But I knew it wasn't. I had to say the words I'd been rehearsing since last night. "I want you to be happy, Mom. That's the most important thing to me. If marrying Mai's dad is going to make you happy, I think you should do it."

Mom hugged me again. "You sure about that?"

I wasn't going to lie to her. "I don't know if Mai's dad and I will ever be good friends. We're pretty different. But I don't think we'll be enemies either." I smiled at Mom and added, "Besides, anyone who loves my Mom can't be all that bad."

"And what about Mai?"

I looked over to where Mai had fallen asleep next to her dad. "I think Mai would make a great sister."

It was an odd feeling as we flew home a few days later. Here I was, warm and dry. I had more food given to me than I could eat. I was going HOME. And all the people I cared about were alive. I couldn't say that for so many others.

Sometimes I try to remember the good things too. How people helped each other out. How I found good friends in Mai, Kasem and one mongrel dog. How, against all odds, I found my mom.

But I'm not sure that I'll ever be able to forget the horrors of the tsunami. Even now, when I close my eyes, the dead faces come back to me. Will I ever be able to look at the sea the same way as I used to? Will I always wonder about the next wave? Will I always be worried that some gang will grab Mai?

I know that I left a part of me behind. Part of me was washed up like the bodies on that beach. It was as if I used to live in a cocoon, all safe and comfy. If I saw a news report about a disaster, I'd just change the channel. Nothing like that could happen to me.

Now I know how wrong I was.

I learned later that more than 230,000 people lost their lives. At least that's how many they think died. So many were washed out to sea that they'll never really know.

Mai's dad's name is Alak and he has a big family in Patong Beach. They lost almost everything in a few short hours. Still, they're planning to rebuild. After Alak gets well again, he's going back to help his family start over. They're going to find a way of reclaiming what nature stole from them.

I admire him for that. I almost feel guilty that I

have such a rich life to return to.

Even better, Alak's family has offered to share what they have with our friend Kasem . . . and one flea-bitten dog.

Some day soon Mai and I will be going back to Patong Beach. We had a long talk with Mom and Alak about it. It just doesn't seem right that we've got so much to go home to . . . when so many others have nothing.

Alak says we have to finish our school year. And, of course, there's the wedding too. I'll be walking my mom down the aisle as soon as Alak is well enough. But come June, I'm going back. I know I'm only one person. But important things always start with one person. Maybe, if enough of us pitch in, we can clean up and rebuild. Maybe together we can take back what those monster waves stole from the people of Patong Beach.

Other HIP Xtreme titles to look for

Hostage

by ALEX KROPP

Rob was just making a bank deposit when the robbers burst in. Soon he's one of six hostages down on the floor, trying to keep the trigger-happy bank robbers from losing control. At the end, Rob is the only hostage left – his life hanging by a thread.

Lost

by SHARON JENNINGS

Rafe Reynolds thought it would be easy to lead a group of kids into wilderness camping. But soon he's lost in the woods with one of the campers. Together they have to deal with everything from bears and broken bones to anger and fist fights.

Overboard

by E.L. THOMAS

An accident at sea leaves Tanner in a lifeboat with his kid sister and a guy he really despises. The survival of the group depends on their working together. But as the hot sun beats down and the water runs out, their chances don't look good.

Quake

by ALEX KROPP

When the first earthquake hits, Cyrus is still at home. He leads his sister to safety, then heads to the local hospital to help other victims. That's when the aftershock hits – the second quake that buries him alive.